Postman Pat

Postman Pat® at the Seaside

Gráinseach an Déin
Deansgrange Library
Tel: 2850860

BAINTE DEN STOC

WITHDRAWN FROM
DÚN LAOGHAIRE-RATHDOWN COUNTY
LIBRARY STOCK

SIMON AND SCHUSTER

Leabharlanna Dhún Laoghaire · Ráth An Dúin

It was a hot day in Greendale. Jess was sunning himself on the bonnet of Pat's van.

"Phew! Come on, Jess," said Pat. "We've got two bags of post to deliver!"

Pat's first stop was the station cafe. He had a postcard for Meera.

"It's from cousin Sanjay!" cried Meera. "He's at the seaside! Can we go to the seaside, Mum?"

"It's too far to go just for the day, Meera," said Nisha.

"Well, I'm sure you'll find something else to do!" smiled Pat, sipping his tea.

While Pat was in the cafe, Ted Glen was getting into a real pickle. He hit a bump in the road and all the sand tipped out of his truck! "Oh 'eck!" he groaned.

PC Selby was scooping up the sand with his helmet when Pat appeared.

"It can't stay here, Ted," PC Selby muttered. "It makes the place look untidy."

"The question is, how are we going to move it?" asked Ted.

"Well you won't move much sand like that!" chuckled Pat. "Tell you what, let's use these spare mailbags."

They started filling the bags with sand, but it poured out of the bottom!

"Oh dear, that's no good," grumbled Pat. And then he caught sight of Reverend Timms wheeling his wheelbarrow across the churchyard. "Hmm, I've got an idea."

Ajay had also had an idea – a family picnic. The Bains set off for Thompson Ground.

"Here we are!" smiled Ajay. "The perfect spot!"

Just then they heard a loud buzzing sound.

"Er, Dad, what's that noise?" asked Meera.

"It's getting louder!" said Nisha.

Suddenly a mysterious veiled figure appeared from behind the hedge. It was Dorothy Thompson, dressed in her beekeeper's clothing.

"I'm afraid you can't have your picnic here," she told them. "Didn't you see the beehives? We're building a proper stand for them, when Ted gets here with the sand. Why don't you go up to Greendale Farm instead?

On the village green, Pat and Ted were in a spot of bother. They'd filled the vicar's wheelbarrow with sand – and then the wheel fell off!

"Now what!" moaned Ted.

"Aha!" said Pat. "I hear a vacuum cleaner. I wonder . . ."

When Sara and Julian passed by on their way to Charlie's, Pat was about to suck up the sand with Dr Gilbertson's vacuum cleaner!

"Are you sure it'll work, Pat?" asked Ted doubtfully.

"I've got a better idea, Dad," called Julian. "Stay right there!"

Julian got on the phone to his friends.

"That's right, Charlie. You tell Tom and Katy, and I'll call Lucy. See you there – and don't forget your bucket and spade!"

Meanwhile the Bains had arrived at Greendale Farm, and their picnic was all ready.

"At last!" sighed Meera.

"That walking's made me hungry!" said Ajay. "Let's eat!"

Ajay was just about to bite into his sandwich, when . . .

Baaa! A flock of sheep came to join their picnic!

"Go away! Shoo!" shouted Ajay, but the sheep wouldn't budge.

"It's no good, Ajay," said Nisha, "we'll have to go somewhere else."

They trudged up to the top of Greendale Hill.

"Phew, it's steep," puffed Meera.

"At least there aren't any sheep," smiled Nisha.

"Or bees!" joked Meera.

But soon there was no picnic either! When Ajay took off his backpack, it rolled down the hill, spilling their food as it went.

"I give up!" groaned Ajay.

Back in Greendale, everyone watched anxiously as the vacuum cleaner got fuller and fuller . . . and fuller and then . . . BOOM! The bag burst, showering them all with sand.

"Uh-oh!" sighed PC Selby. "Looks like we'll have to use my helmet after all!"

But Julian and his friends had other plans! They arrived with their buckets and spades.

"I've brought some friends to play, Dad. Right everyone, get digging!"

"But Julian . . . wait!" gasped Pat.

"This is like being at the seaside," laughed Charlie.

"Now that gives me the best idea yet!" grinned Pat.

In no time at all, Ted Glen's sand was spread across the green, and with deckchairs, umbrellas, a paddling pool and a volleyball net, it was just like the seaside!

Making their way home from their disastrous picnic, the Bains were amazed when they reached the village green.

"What on earth?" said Ajay.

"Wow!" gasped Meera.

"Well," chuckled Pat. "If the Bains can't get to the seaside, the seaside must come to the Bains!"

And everyone had a really brilliant day at Greendale-on-sea!

SIMON AND SCHUSTER
First published in 2006 in Great Britain by Simon & Schuster UK Ltd
Africa House, 64-78 Kingsway
London WC2B 6AH

Postman Pat® © 2006 Woodland Animations, a division of Entertainment Rights PLC
Licensed by Entertainment Rights PLC
Original writer John Cunliffe
From the original television design by Ivor Wood
Royal Mail and Post Office imagery is used by kind permission of Royal Mail Group plc
All rights reserved

Text by Alison Ritchie © 2006 Simon & Schuster UK Ltd

All rights reserved including the right of reproduction in whole or in part in any form

A CIP catalogue record for this book is available from the British Library upon request

ISBN 1 416 91076 X

Printed in China

1 3 5 7 9 10 8 6 4 2